MINI CLASSICS
THE
WALRUS
AND THE
CARPENTER
And Other Nonsense Verse

BY LEWIS CARROLL
ILLUSTRATED BY DOUGLAS CAMERON

‖ ∙PARRAGON∙ ‖

TITLES IN SERIES I AND III OF THE
MINI CLASSICS INCLUDE:

SERIES I

Aladdin and the Magic Lamp
Ali Baba and the Forty Thieves
Alice in Wonderland
A Child's Garden of Verses
Cinderella
The Emperor's New Clothes
The Frog Prince
Goldilocks and the Three Bears
Hansel and Grettel
The Happy Prince
The Little Mermaid
Mother Goose's Rhymes
The Owl and the Pussycat (and other Nonsense Verse)
Puss in Boots
Sleeping Beauty
Snow White and the Seven Dwarfs
The Town Mouse and the Country Mouse (and other
    Aesop's Fables)
The Three Little Pigs
The Ugly Duckling
The Wizard of Oz

SERIES III

Alice Through the Looking-Glass
Brer Rabbit's Riding Horse (and other Stories)
Brer Rabbit and the Turtle Race (and other Stories)
The Cat that Walked by Himself
The Elephant's Child (and How the Camel got his Hump)
The Fox without a Tail (and other Aesop's Fables)
The Golden Goose
Hush-a-Bye Baby (A Collection of Prayers
    and Lullabies)
The Little Match-Girl (and The Swineherd)
A Little Princess
Peter and the Wolf
Peter Pan
The Pied Piper of Hamelin
The Princess and the Pea (and The Red Shoes)
The Remarkable Rocket
Rumpelstiltskin
The Sorcerer's Apprentice
Tom Thumb
Wind in the Willows III – The Adventures of Toad
Wind in the Willows IV – Return to Toad Hall

A PARRAGON BOOK

Published by
Parragon Books,
Unit 13-17, Avonbridge Trading Estate,
Atlantic Road, Avonmouth, Bristol BS11 9QD

Produced by
The Templar Company plc,
Pippbrook Mill, London Road, Dorking, Surrey RH4 1JE

Copyright © 1994 Parragon Book Service Limited

Designed by Mark Kingsley-Monks

Printed and bound in Great Britain

ISBN 1-85813-753-5

THE WALRUS AND THE CARPENTER

The sun was shining
on the sea,
Shining with all his might:
He did his very best to make
The billows smooth and
bright —
And this was odd, because it
was the middle of the night

The moon was shining sulkily,
Because she thought the sun
Had got no business
to be there
After the day was done —
"It's very rude of him,"
she said,
"To come and spoil the fun!"

The sea was wet as wet
could be,
The sands were dry as dry.
You could not see
a cloud, because
No cloud was in the sky:
No birds were flying
overhead —
There were no birds to fly.

The Walrus and the Carpenter
Were walking close at hand;
They wept like anything
to see
Such quantities of sand:
"If this were only
cleared away,"
They said, "it *would*
be grand!"

"If seven maids with
seven mops
Swept it for half a year,
Do you suppose,"
the Walrus said,
"That they could get it clear?"
"I doubt it," said
the Carpenter,
And shed a bitter tear.

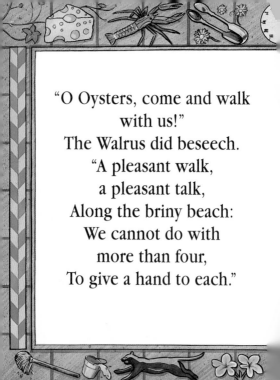

"O Oysters, come and walk
with us!"
The Walrus did beseech.
"A pleasant walk,
a pleasant talk,
Along the briny beach:
We cannot do with
more than four,
To give a hand to each."

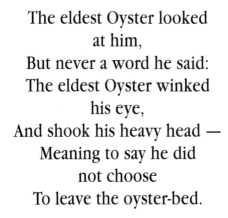

The eldest Oyster looked
at him,
But never a word he said:
The eldest Oyster winked
his eye,
And shook his heavy head —
Meaning to say he did
not choose
To leave the oyster-bed.

But four young Oysters
hurried up,
All eager for the treat:
Their coats were brushed,
their faces washed,
Their shoes were clean
and neat —
And this was odd, because,
you know,
They hadn't any feet.

Four other Oysters
followed them,
And yet another four;
And thick and fast they came
at last,
And more, and more,
and more —
All hopping through the
frothy waves,
And scrambling to the shore.

The Walrus and
the Carpenter
Walked on a mile or so,
And then they rested
on a rock
Conveniently low:
And all the little
Oysters stood
And waited in a row.

"The time has come,"
the Walrus said,
"To talk of many things:
Of shoes — and ships —
and sealing wax —
Of cabbages — and kings —
And why the sea is boiling hot —
And whether pigs
have wings."

"But wait a bit," the
Oysters cried,
"Before we have our chat;
For some of us are
out of breath,
And all of us are fat!"
"No hurry!" said
the Carpenter.
They thanked him
much for that.

"A loaf of bread,"
the Walrus said,
"Is what we chiefly need:
Pepper and vinegar besides
Are very good indeed —
Now if you're ready,
Oysters dear,
We can begin to feed."

"But not on us!" the
Oysters cried,
Turning a little blue.
"After such kindness,
that would be
A dismal thing to do!"
"The night is fine," the
Walrus said.
"Do you admire the view?"

"It was so kind of
you to come!
And you are very nice!"
The Carpenter said
nothing but
"Cut us another slice:
I wish you were not
quite so deaf —
I've had to ask you twice!"

"It seems a shame," the
Walrus said,
"To play them such a trick,
After we've brought them
out so far,
And made them trot
so quick!"
The Carpenter said
nothing but
"The butter's spread
too thick!"

"I weep for you," the
Walrus said,
"I deeply sympathize."
With sobs and tears
he sorted out
Those of the largest size,
Holding his
pocket-handkerchief
Before his streaming eyes.

"O Oysters," said the Carpenter,
"You've had a pleasant run!
Shall we be trotting
home again?"
But answer came
there none —
And this was scarcely odd,
because
They'd eaten every one.

A-SITTING ON A GATE

I'll tell thee everything I can;
There's little to relate.
I saw an aged aged man,
A-sitting on a gate.
"Who are you, aged man?"
I said.
"And how is it you live?"
And his answer trickled
through my head
Like water through a sieve.

He said, "I look for butterflies
That sleep among the wheat:
I make them into mutton-pies,
And sell them in the street.
I sell them unto men,"
he said,
"Who sail on stormy seas;
And that's the way
I get my bread —
A trifle, if you please."

But I was thinking
of a plan
To dye one's whiskers green,
And always use so large a fan
That they could not be seen.
So, having no reply to give
To what the old man said,
I cried, "Come, tell me how
you live!"
And thumped him
on the head.

His accents mild took up
the tale:
He said "I go my ways,
And when I find
a mountain-rill,
I set it in a blaze;
And thence they make
a stuff they call
Rowland's Macassar Oil —
Yet twopence-halfpenny is all
They give me for my toil."

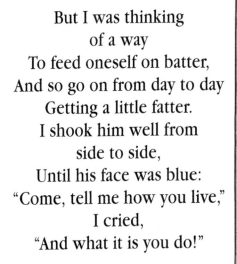

But I was thinking
of a way
To feed oneself on batter,
And so go on from day to day
Getting a little fatter.
I shook him well from
side to side,
Until his face was blue:
"Come, tell me how you live,"
I cried,
"And what it is you do!"

He said, "I hunt for
haddocks' eyes
Among the heather bright,
And work them into
waistcoat-buttons
In the silent night.
And these I do not
sell for gold
Or coin of silvery shine,
But for a copper halfpenny,
And that will purchase nine.

"I sometimes dig for
buttered rolls,
Or set limed twigs for crabs;
I sometimes search the
grassy knolls
For wheels of Hansom-cabs.
And that's the way"
(he gave a wink)
"By which I get my wealth —
And very gladly will I drink
Your Honour's noble health."

I heard him then, for I had just
Completed my design
To keep the Menai bridge
from rust
By boiling it in wine.
I thanked him much
for telling me
The way he got his wealth,
But chiefly for his wish
that he
Might drink my noble health.

And now, if e'er
by chance I put
My fingers into glue,
Or madly squeeze
a right-hand foot
Into a left-hand shoe.
Or if I drop upon my toe
A very heavy weight,
I weep, for it reminds me so,
Of that old man
I used to know —

Whose look was mild, whose
speech was slow,
Whose hair was whiter than
the snow,
Whose face was very like
a crow,
With eyes, like cinders,
all aglow,
Who seemed distracted with
his woe,

Who rocked his body
to and fro,
And muttered mumblingly
and low,
As if his mouth were
full of dough,
Who snorted like a buffalo —
That summer evening
long ago,
A-sitting on a gate.

HOW DOTH THE LITTLE CROCODILE

How doth the little crocodile
Improve his shining tail,
And pour the waters
of the Nile
On every golden scale!

How cheerfully he seems
to grin,
How neatly spreads his claws,
And welcomes little fishes in
With gently smiling jaws!

YOU ARE OLD,
FATHER WILLIAM

"You are old, Father William,"
the young man said,
"And your hair has become
very white;
And yet you incessantly stand
on your head —
Do you think, at your age,
it is right?"

"In my youth," Father William replied to his son, "I feared it might injure the brain; But, now that I'm perfectly sure I have none, Why, I do it again and again."

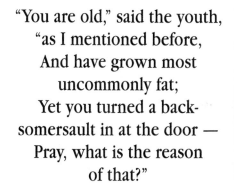

"You are old," said the youth,
"as I mentioned before,
And have grown most
uncommonly fat;
Yet you turned a back-
somersault in at the door —
Pray, what is the reason
of that?"

"In my youth," said the sage,
as he shook his grey locks,
"I kept all my limbs
very supple
By the use of this ointment —
one shilling the box —
Allow me to sell you
a couple?"

"You are old," said the youth,
"and your jaws are too weak
For anything tougher
than suet;
Yet you finished the goose, with
the bones and the beak —
Pray, how did you manage
to do it?"

"In my youth," said his father,
"I took to the law,
And argued each case
with my wife;
And the muscular strength,
which it gave to my jaw,
Has lasted the rest
of my life."

"You are old," said the youth,
"one would hardly suppose,
That your eye was as steady
as ever;
Yet you balanced an eel on
the end of your nose —
What made you so
awfully clever?"

"I have answered three
questions, and that is enough,"
Said his father;
"don't give yourself airs!
Do you think I can listen all
day to such stuff?
Be off, or I'll kick you
downstairs!"

THE LOBSTER QUADRILLE

"Will you walk a little faster?"
said a whiting to a snail.
"There's a porpoise close
behind me, and he's treading
on my tail.

"See how eagerly the lobsters
and the turtles all advance!
They are waiting on the
shingle — will you come
and join the dance?
Will you, won't you, will you,
won't you, will you
join the dance?
Will you, won't you, will you,
won't you, won't you
join the dance?"

"You can really have no notion
how delightful it will be,
When they take us up and
throw us, with the lobsters,
out to sea!"
But the snail replied,
"Too far, too far!"
and gave a look askance —
Said he thanked the whiting
kindly, but he would not join
the dance.

Would not, could not, would
not, could not, would not
join the dance.
Would not, could not, would
not, could not, could not
join the dance.
"What matters it how
far we go?"
his scaly friend replied.
"There is another shore, you
know, upon the other side.

The further off from England
the nearer is to France —
Then turn not pale,
beloved snail, but come
and join the dance.
Will you, won't you, will you,
won't you, will you
join the dance?
Will you, won't you, will you,
won't you, won't you
join the dance?"

THE GARDENER'S SONG

He thought he saw an Elephant,
That practised on a fife:
He looked again,
and found it was
A letter from his wife.
"At length I realise," he said,
"The bitterness of Life!"

He thought he saw a Rattlesnake
That questioned him in Greek:
He looked again,
and found it was
The Middle of Next Week.
"The one thing I regret," he said,
"Is that it cannot speak!"

He thought he saw
a Buffalo
Upon the chimney-piece:
He looked again,
and found it was
His Sister's Husband's Niece.
"Unless you leave this house,"
he said,
"I'll send for the Police!"

He thought he saw
a Banker's Clerk
Descending from the bus:
He looked again,
and found it was
A Hippopotamus:
"If this should stay to dine,"
he said,
"There won't be much for us!"

He thought he saw a Kangaroo
That worked a coffee-mill:
He looked again,
and found it was
A vegetable-Pill.
"Were I to swallow this," he said,
"I should be very ill!"

He thought he saw
a Coach-and-Four
That stood beside his bed:
He looked again,
and found it was
A Bear without a Head.
"Poor thing," he said,
"poor silly thing!
It's waiting to be fed!"

He thought he saw an Albatross
That fluttered round the lamp:
He looked again,
and found it was
A Penny-Postage-Stamp.
"You'd best be getting home,"
he said:
"The nights are very damp!"

He thought he saw
a Garden-Door
That opened with a key:
He looked again,
and found it was
A Double Rule of Three:
"And all its mystery," he said,
"Is clear as day to me!"

TURTLE SOUP

Beautiful Soup,
so rich and green,
Waiting in a hot tureen!
Who for such dainties
would not stoop?
Soup of the evening,
beautiful Soup!

Soup of the evening,
beautiful Soup!
Beau-ootiful Soo-oop!
Beau-ootiful Soo-oop!
Soo-oop of the e-e-evening,
Beautiful, beautiful Soup!

Beautiful Soup!
Who cares for fish,
Game, or any other dish!
Who would not give
all else for two
pennyworth only of
beautiful Soup?
Pennyworth only of
beautiful Soup?
Beau-ootiful Soo-oop!
Beau-ootiful Soo-oop!
Soo-oop of the e-e-evening,
Beautiful, beauti-FUL SOUP!

JABBERWOCKY

'Twas brillig, and
the slithy toves
Did gyre and gimble in
the wabe;
All mimsy were
the borogoves,
And the mome
raths outgrabe.

"Beware the Jabberwock,
my son!
The jaws that bite, the claws
that catch!
Beware the Jubjub bird,
and shun
The frumious Bandersnatch!"

He took his vorpal sword
in hand:
Long time the manxome foe
he sought —
So rested he by
the Tumtum tree,
And stood awhile in thought.

And as in uffish thought
he stood,
The Jabberwock, with eyes
of flame,
Came whiffling through
the tulgey wood,
And burbled as it came!

One, two! One, two!
And through and through
The vorpal blade went
snicker-snack!
He left it dead, and with
its head
He went galumphing back.

"And hast though slain
the Jabberwock?
Come to my arms, my
beamish boy!
O frabjous day! Callooh!
Callay!"
He chortled in his joy.

'Twas brillig, and
the slithy toves
Did gyre and gimble in
the wabe;
All mimsy were
the borogoves,
And the mome
raths outgrabe.

LEWIS CARROLL

Lewis Carroll was the pen-name of
Charles Dodgson (1832-98), a writer best
known for his children's stories, *Alice's Adventures
in Wonderland* and *Alice Through the Looking-
Glass.* His wonderful nonsense verse has inspired
many different illustrators over the years but the
first man to illustrate *The Walrus and the Carpenter*
played an important part in its history.
Apparently, Lewis Carroll could not decide
which companion to give the walrus and so left
the choice up to the artist, Sir John Tenniel.
He had three alternatives: a butterfly,
a baronet or a carpenter, and luckily
Sir John decided he would have most fun
drawing the carpenter together with the walrus,
otherwise we would have been left with
The Walrus and the Baronet!